MIDNIGHT TAXI MADNESS

Part 1

M.A. SHAH

DEDICATION

To my little twin boys,
Syed Ismail Haider & Syed Suliman Haider
I cannot wait to see you grow up with the full support of my
beautiful wife, your Mummy.

TABLE OF CONTENTS

ACKNOWLEDGEMENTS

I'd like to thank my family, who have supported me a lot, especially my Mum, who encouraged me to go ahead with this book.

INTRODUCTION

You must have heard numerous stories about people switching careers and venturing into completely new fields of work. This story, however, is a bit different. It's about a career shift that taught me not just about resilience and adaptability but also about the various shades of human nature – the good and the bad, the happy and the sad.

This journey isn't just about a change in profession; it's about embracing change and finding balance during the most challenging times. My story moves from flipping through accounting ledgers to navigating the roads of Benfleet, highlighting personal growth, community connection, and the relentless pursuit of fulfilling work in a rapidly evolving world.

My name is Mohammed Ali Shah. I've been an accountant for the past seven years, moving from a practice in the accountancy field to the industry sector. I worked my way up, eventually joining Amazon Audible in what became my last role in this career. COVID-19 played a significant role in changing my life; while working from home during the lockdown, I grew bored and decided to pursue a side job.

I decided to venture into taxi driving, and now, I work as an ABC taxi driver in Benfleet, within the borough of Castle Point Castle. I'm originally from South End on Sea, where I currently reside, but my work in Benfleet is quite a manageable commute, about six to seven miles from South End, so it is not much of a hassle either.

My schedule, though? That's the complete opposite.

It is quite demanding, balancing night duties as a taxi driver seven days a week with my accountancy job. My day typically starts with the accountancy work at around nine o'clock, sometimes as early as half past eight. I work as an accountant until about half past five in the evening. Then, immediately, without even a minute's break (not exactly, but you get the point), I transition to my taxi driving duties.

So, needless to say, my daily routine is quite a marathon. On weekdays, Monday through Thursday, I wrap up my accountancy job around 5:30 PM and immediately shift to taxi driving, continuing until 1:00 AM. Fridays and Saturdays are even more packed. I start taxi driving at 5:00 PM and keep going until about 5:30 the next morning. Then, on Saturdays, I begin again at either 11:00 or 11:30 in the morning, continuing straight through until 5:30 PM. Sundays are no less hectic, with my taxi shift running from about 10:00 AM all the way to 1:00 AM the following morning. This schedule means I'm working a heck of a lot of hours with hardly any breaks. In fact, I only take a day off in case of unforeseen circumstances. So, being a cab driver for me is essentially almost a 24/7 commitment.

Doesn't seem so easy, now, does it?

We have a lot of sociable hours and unsociable hours. For example, sociable hours for us are when we have customers. That's our time for speaking to the customer, listening to their opinions, and seeing whatever happens. Those are our sociable hours. Then, we also have what we call unsociable hours, which is when we're waiting for a ride. During these times, we usually line up in queues and wait. This waiting period could be a short five-minute wait or even extend to two hours. The length of these waits mostly depends on the day's dynamics and the overall busyness.

It's quite interesting how the whole taxi setup operates. Speaking as an ABC taxi driver, I'm actually a private hire driver, which means I can only pick up rides that are booked through our office or the app. The rides vary, ranging from very short journeys to much longer ones. Our taxi meter starts at a £3 fare in the morning, lasting until nine o'clock. After nine, we switch to tariff two, starting at £4. And after midnight, it's £5. So, the starting price of our taxi varies at different hours.

The shortest ride I've had was less than 50 yards, where the meter hadn't even moved. I was taking an elderly person who obviously couldn't walk, so it made sense. That's the shortest journey I've encountered. On the other hand, the longest ride I've taken to date involved multiple cities: from Leicester to Norwich, then to Nottingham, and up north, covering really long distances. We're talking about journeys lasting several hours, like four or five hours, to places like Manchester and Birmingham.

We take very long rides as well every once in a while. Of course, this depends on how alert and mentally prepared we are. As a cab driver, it's not just about being responsible for your own safety; you also have to ensure the safety of your passengers. This is crucial because all sorts of things can happen on the road, and you have to be alert all the time to tackle any unforeseen situation; it is a matter of seconds, and everything can change. So, it's critical to understand that as a cab driver, having a good amount of sleep is essential. This ensures that you can handle long rides easily without the risk of feeling sleepy during the drive. If you ever feel tired, don't hesitate or think twice—immediately sign out, go offline, and head home. Your life and your passengers' lives are far more important than earning extra money. For instance, I work many hours, but since I make sure that I sleep well and rest before I hit the road, I am one of the happiest and most jovial cab drivers in our area and remarkably active compared to others. My customers love me, and this is reflected in their reviews.

There have been moments at the ABC office, too. They once called me into the office to proudly share how satisfied my customers were. Hearing those positive comments truly boosts my enthusiasm and love for this job. But this doesn't mean it's an easy job. In fact, I find being a taxi driver to be one of the hardest jobs. It's not as easy as people might think. Receiving good customer reviews and appreciation from the company is what keeps us motivated and striving to do our best.

Talking about the timings, we have our busy hours too when it becomes difficult to simply enjoy what we do. Typically, Mondays through Thursdays are quieter. However, lately, Thursdays in Benfleet are turning almost as hectic as Fridays, although they still don't compare to the actual chaos experienced on Fridays and Saturdays, which are our busiest days. And they're the main days when we have to work hard. Because if we don't work hard on those days, we won't be able to cover up the money and basically make a decent living.

That means sometimes, even during a normal weekday shift, for example, an eight-hour shift on a Friday or Saturday, I might end up working a double shift. Not all drivers do this, but I do. On weekends, I often work double shifts. I've even worked up to 16 hours at a stretch. The longest shift I've done was 21 hours on a Saturday night. I chose to work these extended hours because there were fewer drivers available, and it was crucial for some of us to stay out for emergencies. This was particularly important during COVID-19, which had a significant impact on taxi services. Ambulances could take as long as 48 hours to arrive, so in emergencies, people couldn't wait that long. So, there came handy services such as taxis, helping people get to their destinations quicker and more efficiently.

So, we have all sorts of things happening around taxi service. People prefer it because of the high privacy and convenience it provides. Normally, people use buses too as a cheaper option, but some people prefer luxury, especially when they can afford it for their conveyance. Sometimes, people use taxis for special or emergency situations, so that gives them the benefit of getting to their destination faster than any other public transport. If, for example, the train service is not working or public transport such as a bus is not available, people know they can always resort to a taxi. It's become a reliable fallback option. But some people regularly use taxis as their primary means of transportation, because it just makes their life a bit easier. And obviously, they're a bit more fluent money-wise and prioritize convenience.

In our area, there are numerous taxi companies, but ABC stands out as a well-known and recognized service in Benfleet. The locals here consistently choose ABC local cabs over Uber, showing a strong preference for our service. Naturally, there's a sense of rivalry, as Uber is also a popular choice for some, making it our biggest competitor. We're not particularly fond of Uber as it kind of nicks our jobs; it's a classic case of local cabs versus Uber. But still, I think people in our area rather prefer their local cabs; they feel safer and find their local cabs more convenient.

So this was a little overview of how taxi services work in Benfleet. But this book is more about the stories, focusing on the experiences I've had as a cab driver. And let me tell you, those experiences were life-changing for me, ranging from entertaining and emotional to sometimes traumatic. As a cab driver, I've encountered a whole new side of the world, experiencing its diverse spectrum. And I am eager to share all those stories with my readers, hoping they, too, will get to learn a lot of things from them.

I've been taking a taxi for over two years now, and the reason why I chose it was that I believe a taxi is a very important aspect of public transport. Although I had not expected it to turn out like that, my time as a taxi driver has taught me a great deal about life, people, and various facets of the human experience. I don't believe I could have had such a diverse experience in any other job. It is a new experience every day.

The things I learned before I became a cab driver were beyond my imagination. In this book, I'll share some of the most impactful experiences and situations I've encountered. From a public transport perspective, taxis offer a unique overview. We pick up people from all walks of life, encompassing all ages and genders – from young children to elderly individuals and from the poorest to the wealthiest multimillionaires. I've even come across quite a few celebrities as my customers as well! But as a taxi driver, it was different. I was not raving about them upon seeing them, considering I was on duty. And, of course, in a taxi, it just becomes a very, very strange bond, a relationship between customers and the driver that you will get to read in the following chapters.

Get ready for the longest cab ride on this journey with me as your driver. Hope you will enjoy it as much as I did sharing it with you!

CHAPTER 01

I'll begin with my very first story, a particularly traumatic one. This story takes me back to around a year and a half ago. I clearly remember it was a Wednesday. The incident occurred while I was at work. My task was to pick up a customer from the Benfleet Tandoori parlor, a restaurant, and take him to Basildon, London. It was table nine that had ordered the cab, and the journey was estimated to be between 22 to 25 minutes. As I waited for the customer, I was wondering whether it would be a male or female. But when the passenger arrived, it was a male who sat in the front with me.

I didn't know the exact location where I had to take him. I greeted him warmly, asking, "Hello, my friend. How's it going? How are you? Are you keeping well?" I even mentioned my own pleasant experience at the Benfleet Tandoori parlor. However, the man seemed quite grumpy and uninterested in chatting, responding dismissively with, "Yeah, it's alright."

Realizing his mood, I decided it was better to stay quiet. I thought to myself, he seems to be in a bad mood and quite irritable. So, I simply asked him for the exact location in Basildon we were headed to, saying, "So my friend, where exactly in Basildon are we going?"

He wouldn't tell me the exact location. He said, "Just take me over to Basildon, and I'll tell you where once we're there. I will guide you from there." He didn't say 'guide,' though. He said, 'I will tell you where to go from there.' He was basically mentoring me.

I responded to him, saying it would be easier if he just gave me a postcode or an address so I could take him straight to the destination. But it seemed like the guy didn't want to give his address, and for some reason, I couldn't understand. He insisted, "Just drive to Basildon, and I'll guide you from there." When he didn't budge, I decided to just go with the flow.

I felt quite awkward and uncomfortable. He appeared to be a very moody person, not keen on speaking. Honestly, he also seemed a bit vicious. His manner of speaking, the way he sat, everything about him screamed 'weird.' As a cab driver, I've seen all sorts of people, and I've learned to distinguish between the nice, decent folks and those who are violent, dangerous, or angry.

So, I started driving and reassured him, "Don't worry, my friend. I'll take you straight to Basildon, and you can guide me from there if you like. No problem. But ultimately, it's important for me to know how to get there. So, I'm going to take you straight to Basildon, and you can guide me from there." He grunted, which I took as a 'yes,' and we began our journey.

I stayed quiet as we drove. Then, suddenly, the guy started speaking. He initiated the conversation with, "You know I am a very dangerous man."

A bit perplexed, I glanced at him and then back at the road, asking, "I beg your pardon?"

He reiterated, "You heard me. I said I'm a very dangerous person."

I responded, "Okay," not really knowing what else to say.

He then said, "Yeah, I'll tell you something about myself."

Still apprehensive and a bit confused, I encouraged him, "Go on, you can tell me. Feel free to share anything." I smiled, half believing he was just joking with me.

But the story he told next shook me to the core.

He revealed, "I have committed a murder, and I never got caught for it."

Trying to keep my composure, I could only utter, "Oh." I was at a loss for words, unsure how to react. Honestly, the way I felt at that moment is hard to explain. It was a very strange sensation, still vivid in my memory, as if it happened yesterday.

His tone was serious and monotonous as he told me this, which was pretty scary. Just imagine him sitting beside me, claiming he had committed a murder. It might have been a joke, but my instincts suggested otherwise. I knew better than to ignore such feelings, yet there was still a chance he was lying and messing with me. However, as he continued the conversation, detailing exactly how he did it and what he had done, my instincts told me he wasn't lying.

I'll share exactly what happened next and what he said.

He told me again that he had committed a murder about 15 or 16 years ago, living in London at the time. He had a brother whose friend, living in the same building, stabbed his brother. It was a minor stab in the arm. He didn't give names, so I only knew the bare details of who stabbed whom, and I wasn't eager to know more.

He continued, telling me that he was infuriated upon hearing about the stabbing. So, he went to his brother's friend's home, got inside, and killed the guy. He then said he threw him off the top of the building, resulting in his death. He wasn't sure if anyone saw him do it, but he claimed that no one dared to report him because they were too scared.

Then, looking at me with challenging eyes, he added, "No one reported it because they were scared of me." The whole situation was too much for me. I was thinking, 'Whoa, what's happening here?'

Before I had time to fully grasp what he was saying, he went on to describe what he did with the body. He said he took the body far up north, a six-and-a-half-hour journey, but didn't specify the location. He didn't tell me where exactly, and I didn't know what I would have done with that information anyway. He told me he threw the body, packed in a black bag, in a lake.

I was panicking, thinking, 'Oh my God, this guy might kill me. What do I do?!' My mind raced as I remembered he never gave me the exact drop-off location and kept stalling. He didn't give me a postcode or a specific location. It seemed like a dead end, and I was very scared. This guy could do anything.

Unable to find the right words in response to everything he had told me, I mustered all the courage I had and said to him, "My friend, you're a very good man. You know what? I'm going to give you a free lift." I was hoping that I hadn't upset him earlier by talking too much. Offering the free ride was a desperate attempt on my part to make it out of this ride alive.

To my surprise, the guy declined my offer, saying, "No. I'm going to pay you. I appreciate hard workers who make a living for themselves."

I nodded, managing a forced smile, and kept driving, eager to reach the destination as soon as possible. Thankfully, the rest of the ride was uneventful, though I remained half-focused on the man next to me, who had just confessed to being a murderer.

When the ride ended, he unexpectedly gave me a hefty tip. It was something I hadn't anticipated. Despite giving me the fright of my life, he compensated me with a generous tip. The fare was around 26 quid, but he handed me a 50-pound note. So, that was nearly a 24-pound tip!

I was both amazed and scared. This man could have done anything to me; he could have killed me. His demeanor seemed like that of a cold-blooded murderer, though perhaps I was influenced by the story he had told. I'm still not sure if what he told me was true or not, but I have decided to let it stay a mystery. I don't want to get myself into trouble, and I strictly adhere to my firm's policy of not sharing customer details. I certainly don't want any trouble with someone like him.

This experience is one of those stories I found worth sharing. As a cab driver, sitting with someone who claimed to be a cold-blooded murderer is a big deal. I didn't pry further or report him. I didn't have any information on him, as he booked the ride from a restaurant and didn't give me an exact drop-off location. He just had me drive to a dead-end street, and he walked the rest from there.

So, even if I wanted to report him, I couldn't. Honestly, I was so terrified by the encounter that I didn't work for two and a half weeks afterward. That's how traumatized I was. I had no way of knowing if the guy was telling the truth, but my instincts told me he wasn't lying. The way he told the story didn't sound like it was made up. You just never know.

CHAPTER 02

About eight months ago, I had an interesting ride. I was scheduled to pick up a passenger from a very famous pub, Hoy & Helmet, in Benfleet. This pub is well-known because it draws people from various places, some traveling from distant areas and others from nearby, not to mention the locals from Benfleet. The ride was booked by a woman named Hannah.

Upon arrival, it wasn't long before I saw Hannah exiting the pub with a guy. They both got into the back of my vehicle. Following my usual routine, I greeted them, asked about their evening, and asked if they had enjoyed themselves. They responded nicely, telling me that they had a good time. Nodding, I then inquired about their drop-off location, given it was not mentioned at the time of booking. It was a late Saturday night, around 1 AM, and they were both visibly drunk and tipsy, taking a moment to reply. They informed me they needed to go to different locations, which wasn't a problem as it sometimes happens, and I began the ride with the destination that was nearest first.

Hannah informed me that she lived in Gray's, and the guy lived in Purfleet. I was fine with this since the two locations were relatively close to each other, about 10-15 minutes apart. However, they were still quite a distance from the pub where I picked them up. I calculated the total journey would take us around 45 minutes, likely extending to an hour because I needed to drop Hannah off at Gray's first, which would take 35 minutes, followed by an additional 15 minutes to drop the guy off in Purfleet.

With the long drive ahead, I began the journey. At some point, I realized I didn't even know the guy's name. To pass the time, I engaged them in casual conversation about their evening, to which they enthusiastically replied, "Yeah, we had a smashing night out tonight."

I nodded and smiled, initially assuming they were a couple based on their behavior. However, as the conversation unfolded, it became apparent they hardly knew each other. Their discussion revealed they had likely just met, given the way they were inquiring about basic details of each other's lives. It dawned on me how awkward the situation was, as they were quite lovey-dovey with each other despite being almost strangers.

The girl started to ask the guy questions on random topics, such as where he lived and how long he had lived in Purfleet. The guy reciprocated with similar questions. It was clear they had just met, probably somewhere in the hallway of the pub where I had picked them up.

I was a bit taken aback by their friendliness, especially considering the late hour and the fact they were complete strangers to each other. But again, it wasn't a complete surprise as these things happened in such places quite often. So, I shrugged it off and continued to drive.

A few minutes later, we were out of Benfleet and now on the motorway. That's when things started to get a little awkward. I had no idea what was happening in the back of my car since I was focused on the road. It was a motorway, so I couldn't take any risks. But when it got dead silent in the back, it made me wonder if everything was okay. The first thought that crossed my mind was that they both had passed out. They were both tipsy when I picked them up, so it was quite possible they were knocked out in the back seat. However, my guess was wrong when I started to hear some noise. I tried to look in the rear mirror to see what was happening, but all I could see was a foot in the air in the back seat. Not long after, a red heel sailed over my shoulder before landing in my lap.

Then, the reality of the situation dawned on me, and I couldn't help but find it both absurd and amusing. Judging by the noises and the brief visual I had caught, there was no doubt left: they were having sex right there in my car's backseat!

What shocked me even more was that these total strangers were engaging in full-on sex in the back of the cab. I struggled to keep my laughter in check but somehow managed to maintain a professional tone, saying, "Sorry, you've just dropped your heel." She nonchalantly brushed it off, gesturing towards the seat beside me, which I believed was her way of saying, 'Just put it on the front seat.'

Of course, having sex in the back of someone's car is inappropriate, but I'm not the type of driver to make a scene. I simply complied and placed the heel at the front of the car as instructed.

I was still trying to wrap my head around their boldness. They seemed utterly indifferent to my presence, engrossed in such intimate acts without a hint of shyness. It takes a certain level of brazen confidence to do something that is audacious. To put it mildly, their behavior was NAUGHTY!

Their antics had inevitably distracted me, so I forced myself to disregard whatever was going on in the backseat and concentrate on driving. Before long, we were approaching the girl's house in Gray's. I was at a loss for how to tell them to stop since we had arrived at their destination. Gathering my courage and assuming they would have wrapped up their 'activities' by then, I turned around to inform them that we had reached, and it was time for them to get out of the car.

I wished I hadn't turned around. They were still on their business with no regard to where they were or the driver taking them there! I couldn't believe it. Sometime during the ride, I had even turned on the lights for them, hoping it would help them wrap things up quicker. But no, they were still at it!

Feeling incredibly awkward and unsure of what to do next, I cleared my throat once they were finally done and said, "Look, guys, you just had sex in my car. You have made it smelly, mucky, and dirty. I'm not going to put the next customer in a dirty car. So I'm gonna have to charge you for a full cleaning." That was a surcharge of 70 pounds, which, to my surprise, they were happy to pay. They actually seemed glad that I took them on board and didn't interrupt their...err… activities.

So this was undoubtedly one of the most bizarre, yet amusing, experiences I've encountered on the job. I don't know how to put it in words, but that was just so awkward. I was caught off guard. I had had instances where people would go all passionate and kissing in the back of the car, but sex? That was new to me.

So when I dropped the girl in Gray's, I turned to the next location to drop the guy. I asked the guy if he even knew her. I wanted to check and confirm. I was seeking some kind of explanation or rationale. The guy went on like, "Yeah… I mean, we just met up in the hallway. We had a good time and, well…. ended up sharing this ride." He simply shrugged as if it was nothing out of the ordinary. I nodded and asked if he had her contact number or something. He told me that now that she was gone, he didn't have any way to contact her. They were just strangers and never got to exchange contact details. Just two strangers having a good time and some sex.

I was shocked. Or perhaps I'd just never been exposed to them before, which is why the shock hit me so hard. I didn't know it was such a common thing to do. Shrugging it off, which, by the way, wasn't easy at all, I just went home. The only thing that I wanted to do the first thing after dropping them off was to get the car cleaned. I couldn't continue to drive the dirty car. So, the following day, I got the car fully cleaned before I started work again.

CHAPTER 03

This is one of a kind of an experience that I went through, a very traumatic one if you ask me.

Why?

Well, here is why.

Before I start with this one, I want to tell you that I've signed up with my company for picking up animals. I am more than happy to pick them up. I think not many particularly enjoy picking up four-legged passengers, but that's not me. Many of the company drivers don't pick up dogs or any sort of animals.

I never saw it as a big deal. I mean, what harm could it be?

So, after signing up, I came across this ride that I had to pick up from the high road in Benfleet. The customer booked the ride under the name 'John,' which I think was a lie. His name probably was not John. You will get to know why I thought so.

Well, he ordered a cab under this name. He had a dog that he put beside him when he got in my cab. Of course, being an animal, it couldn't stay still and often moved to my side.

As usual, I greeted the guy with a smile, as I did to all my passengers, and asked him where we were going. He directed me on the route and told me to drive to the South End of Bridgewater near the shops. I knew what he meant and understood the directions clearly. I had seen those shops he was talking about, so it wasn't a problem.

Next, I started our ride toward our destination. We must have been halfway through the journey when the guy mentioned that I would have to bring him back as well. Seeing no issue with that, I shrugged and agreed to bring him back to where I had picked him up from. He didn't say much after that, and I proceeded to drive toward his drop-off location.

During the ride, I could sense that the guy was somewhat moody. He hadn't talked much, but there was something about him that made me think that way. Maybe it was the aura he gave off, the way he carried himself, or simply the lack of conversation. I couldn't put my finger on it, but it was definitely something. Perhaps it was a sixth sense. Being a driver for years sure sharpened my senses.

However, being myself, I tried to strike up a conversation with him. I'm naturally curious about people and enjoy getting to know new faces. It's one of the reasons I like this job. So, when I asked him how he was, his response was just a grunt. That reaction was a clear indication that he wasn't interested in making acquaintances. In fact, it almost seemed like he was avoiding getting too familiar with me. He seemed different.

Obviously, everyone is different from one another, but this one was the dangerous kind. He looked intimidating, and I couldn't shake the feeling that he was involved in something illegal—perhaps a drug dealer or addict.

Either way, I didn't want to get into trouble. I couldn't show that I was scared of him or even suspicious. If my doubts were true, that would only get me into danger. So, I kept driving in silence and finally reached the drop-off point. He went out, leaving his dog in the backseat of the car. I waited for him to come back so I could drop him off at where I had picked him up, as decided.

It was chilly out there, and I was wearing a thick jacket that my mom had gifted to me on my last birthday. It was quite fluffy. So as I waited, and sometime during that, my eyes fell on the rearview mirror, and my breath kind of got caught in my throat.

The dog was just behind my left shoulder, just sitting there still and staring at me. Although I am not usually scared of dogs, this one was pretty big, and the way it was staring at me had me panicking. I sat there, frozen like a statue. I had a feeling that if I moved, it might attack me.

I regretted letting the dog sit in the backseat, feeling it had gotten too close for comfort. I sat there, making sure not to move and somehow trigger it. So I just moved my eyes to look outside, praying that its owner would come soon. To make matters worse, the dog kept growling. I even feared that it might be rabid.

The guy had not taken too long to come, about only 10 minutes. But the wait was excruciating. And before he came back, the dog did what I feared it would because of the way it kept staring at me. The growling got louder, and not soon after, it bit my left shoulder.

Luckily, I was wearing that thick, fluffy jacket, which saved me from losing a meaty chunk of my left shoulder to that scary dog. But honestly, the incident scared my life out of it. I was a little angry, considering that being the dog's owner, my passenger should have known about its behavior and shouldn't have left it inside the car with me. I was pretty sure he was doing drugs somewhere, leaving this terrifying dog with me. I couldn't even get out of the car since the dog wasn't letting go of my jacket. In an effort to escape, I opened the car door, but the owner, seeing what was happening, didn't come to help.

I kept screaming, not knowing if the dog had managed to bite through the thick jacket. I was so scared that I almost felt like crying. The only sensible way out of the situation seemed to be to take my jacket off. I pulled my arm out from the right side and then wriggled it down from my left arm. The dog still had my jacket in its mouth, but luckily, I was out of its clutches. I got out of the car as fast as I could and shut the door behind me. Looking at the owner, who was standing in one of the nearby shops, it seemed he didn't even care about what had happened to me. It was disheartening. I had allowed his dog in my ride, and he couldn't muster any concern for my well-being.

Later, after finishing the ride, I went straight to the hospital. When I took off my shirt, there were marks where the dog had bitten me, and I was bleeding. I had thought it hadn't gotten through the jacket, but I was wrong. That made me wonder what could have happened if I hadn't been wearing it. I might have lost my left arm.

I was traumatized, to say the least. I had never encountered such violent dogs before. The wound was severe enough to require bandaging, not just cleaning. The doctors told me it was serious, and if the dog had been unvaccinated or rabid, I could have faced life-threatening consequences. They gave me a tetanus injection after cleaning the wound, just in case the dog wasn't clean.

That guy, on the other hand, was so rude. Not that I could tell that to his face, given his mood, but I wish I could. When the ride finished, he simply took his dog and left without bothering to apologize, compensate for the damage his dog caused, or even ask if I was okay.

After that day, I decided to avoid picking up dogs for a while. I was fine with smaller pets, but I needed some time to recover from the trauma before I felt ready to transport dogs again. I believe if that guy had been polite enough to ask me how I was doing and helped me with getting the dog away from me, I wouldn't have been so reluctant to start picking up dogs in my cab again.

Eventually, I signed back up to pick up pets because the office needed someone to take rides with pets, and no other driver was willing to do it. Hoping for the best, I decided to place bigger pets in the back boot of the car for safety.

Despite the incident, I committed to these rides, knowing the difficulties customers with pets face in finding transportation. However, I wasn't compensated any extra for it. I did that for the passengers.

CHAPTER 04

This story recounts a deeply emotional experience I had while working as a cab driver, an experience that holds a special place in my heart.

I have a private customer, a couple living in Benfleet named Chris and Michelle. They are the ideal of a happy, loving couple, the kind you dream of meeting when you find your soulmate. Their relationship made you believe in true love, even in modern times.

Michelle is 38 years old, and Chris is 45 years old. They never go out without each other, from what I have noticed from providing them conveyance often. They always go out together on a Friday or Saturday night when I take them; they always go together. They also trust me with their children, picking up and dropping them off, making them my regular private clients.

They're pretty well-off financially, millionaires to be precise, but their behavior is very down to earth, unlike people of their stature, who usually are. That's what I love about them the most. They have around seven different businesses. They have told me about it all themselves during our conversation on the rides. But despite the ups and downs, their love remained steadfast, and they have a beautiful home.

One day, I got a phone call from the missus, Michelle. One thing I want to mention here is that my regular customers call me 'Mo,' which is short for my name 'Mohammad.'

So when she called me, she sounded drunk, but I could understand what she was trying to say. She told me she was at the famous Benfleet pub, Hoy & Helmet, which I've mentioned before in other stories. She was calling me to pick her up from there, and it was clear that she was pretty drunk at the moment. Without wasting much time, I went to pick her up.

When I reached the pub, I saw her outside, sitting on the floor, intoxicated. I got out of the cab right away, walked to her, grabbed her hand, and helped her up. Then, I helped her in walking towards the car and sitting in the front seat. She was so drunk that she could barely speak, but I asked her anyway what had happened. It was unlike her to be in such a state, so I was worried. Plus, she never went out without her husband.

She started crying as if mentioning her husband had triggered a reminder of something painful. She was crying so intensely that I decided to let her vent and speak to her when she was ready. So, without another word, I started to drive her home, which was not too far.

When I felt that she had calmed down a bit, I asked her again, "What happened, Michelle? Is everything okay? Tell me, why are you so upset?"

She didn't answer. I asked her again, "Where is your husband?" And then, it happened again; she started crying. It had been a while since I had last seen her and her husband, so I had no idea how they were doing. So, when she called me after almost a month, specifically to pick her up from a pub she went to without her husband, I was worried. Her crying at the mention of her husband only added to my concern. I felt my heart sinking, imagining the worst.

But knowing that assumptions wouldn't help, I persisted and asked again. Thankfully, she finally opened up about her situation.

"I just found out that Chris has kidney cancer," Michelle revealed, her voice cracking as she struggled to speak.

I was shocked. It took me a minute to absorb the news and understand Michelle's condition.

"I am so sorry, Michelle," I managed to say, but deep down, I was devastated. I couldn't imagine what she was going through. Having seen Chris and Michelle always together and happy, the news hit me hard. I couldn't find the right words to console her.

According to her, his cancer had spread throughout his body. I didn't pry for details, knowing how difficult it must be for her to share all this, but I understood that the situation was bad. I could feel my eyes getting watery and tears threatening to fall, but I kept myself composed.

"Hey... Michelle...," I began, trying to offer some comfort. "He will be alright. Just keep praying. He needs you to be strong right now. And don't forget, you've got three beautiful children who are by your side through this. I know it's tough, but your husband needs you more than ever."

Michelle nodded in understanding, and I hoped my words had given her some solace. I continued to drive and soon reached her home. I got out of the car and helped her out, as she was still quite drunk and struggled to walk without help.

I helped her open the door to her house, and there was her husband, sitting right in front of us on the couch. He looked weaker and older than when I last saw him, which had only been a few weeks ago. It seemed like he had aged years in just those few weeks due to the cancer.

He smiled when he saw me and invited me inside. "Mo, come over here," he said. So, I opened the door wider and assisted Michelle. After helping Michelle to sit, I approached him. He greeted me with a warm smile, which I returned, and then he began to tell me how he was doing. Although Michelle had informed me about his condition, hearing it from Chris himself was a different experience entirely.

He then said, "Mo, I have a favor to ask of you."

I looked at him, nodding, curious about what he might request.

Chris continued, "I want you to be there for my children, to drive them wherever they need to go, whenever they need it."

I understood his wish, knowing the trust he placed in me with his family. However, I explained that my life might take different directions, and I might not always be a cab driver. But I assured him that I would be there for his children as long as I continued driving.

Chris nodded, understanding my position. It was heartbreaking to see such a valued customer, always so vibrant and full of life, now in this condition, fighting for his life.

It seemed he was aware of the gravity of his situation, perhaps understanding he might not have much time left. Yet, he remained as loud and spirited as he was before, trying his best to be the man I had always known before his illness took hold. I've stayed in touch, visiting him at his house every other week or sometimes calling to check in on how he's doing.

Sadly, his condition is only getting worse. The future is uncertain, and amidst all this, being close to his family, I am doing my best to support them in any way they need. I often ponder how his wife will manage everything—the home, the children, and Chris's needs. She has little experience running a business, as Chris has always taken care of it.

The reason I'm sharing this experience with you is to show the other side of my profession. It has connected me with people in the most unexpected ways. I have found a second family in those I've met, sharing in both their joys and sorrows.

This is the beauty of my job; it offers the chance to connect with strangers who can become like family. But it's also a harsh reminder of life's unpredictability.

CHAPTER 05

One day, I had to pick up a ride from the Rayleigh Pink Toothbrush and take them to Benfleet. It wasn't much of a journey, as it's a very short distance. So, I went over to the Pink Toothbrush, as the location mentioned, and waited for the passengers. Soon, three young girls approached my car and got in. They seemed to be teenagers and were probably university students. Two of them sat in the backseat, and one sat in the front.

It wasn't really uncommon to pick up drunk people from that location, so I was kind of expecting them to be drunk. From the looks of it, they weren't too drunk, just a little tipsy and in their senses. Although I don't particularly have a problem picking up drunk passengers, it's always better when they're not since it's easier for me to ask about their destination and understand it better.

So, as they settled inside the car, I greeted them and asked how they were doing. By now, you must have an idea that this is the usual thing I do. I'm a very jolly driver and always want my passengers to have a good and pleasant journey in my cab. They really appreciate that.

I continued on the journey, taking them home. We were on Reily Road in Benfleet, and I was driving at the usual speed. A few minutes went by when, all of a sudden, there was an animal running frantically on the road I was driving on. At first, I couldn't understand what animal it was, but as it neared our car, running almost straight into it, I realized that it was a dog, a pet, it seemed. The way it was running, confused and panicked, it was clear that it was looking for its owner or was bothered by the surroundings.

Seeing the dog running, I slowed down and activated my hazard lights. It was around half past three in the morning, so it was particularly unusual to see a pet dog roaming the roads. I kept my focus on the rearview mirror to ensure there was no car close behind me as I reduced my speed. There was one car at some distance, approaching too fast. I panicked because it seemed the driver was unaware of the dog ahead and was speeding.

I feared the car would overtake mine and hit the dog. In hopes of avoiding this, I steered my car toward the center of the road, hoping the following car would switch to the fast lane and notice the dog. To warn the driver, I waved, hoping he would slow down. Unfortunately, he didn't seem to grasp the situation and decided to overtake me from the right.

Fortunately, he noticed the dog in time to avoid hitting it. I breathed a sigh of relief as he sped off without harming the dog. I then stopped the car and turned to talk to the girls. "Look, guys, we've got to get this dog off the road. Otherwise, someone's going to end up running it over and killing it."

I could tell it was someone's dog that they had lost. There's a certain look to a lost dog, so I tried to shoo it away from the road. Unfortunately, this only made the dog panic more, and it darted to the left side. As it did, we got out of the vehicle and started chasing the dog in hopes of catching it. Our plan was to take a picture of the dog to post online, letting people know it was lost so its owners could come and get it.

But our efforts were in vain as the dog ran into the woods, and we couldn't follow any further. "Well, we tried our best. I hope its owners find it soon. Let me just take you and drop you back home," I told my passengers, who were a bit disappointed for not being able to save the dog.

However, once we got back into the cab, we decided to take a different approach. We downloaded a picture of a similar dog from Google and posted it on Facebook with a caption explaining that we came across a dog in the area that seemed to be lost. We included the location and the road name and described the place where we last saw the dog, hoping this might help in reuniting the dog with its owners.

After our attempts to catch the dog, I decided to call 999, the emergency number, hoping the police could help with the situation. A woman answered, and upon explaining that we had found a lost dog in the area and needed someone to rescue it, she directed me to dial 101 instead.

Unfortunately, I wasn't able to connect with the switchboard or anyone else through that number. In the end, I had no choice but to give up, though I was a bit relieved by the fact that we had made an effort to alert potential rescuers by posting on Facebook.

I'm not sure what happened after that and what became of the dog or whether its owners were ever found, but this incident remains another memorable experience in my career as a cab driver. Encounters like these are common in my line of work, providing me with opportunities to offer help where I can. It's part of what makes my job both challenging and rewarding.

CHAPTER 06

I want to share another story with you. I think this one reflects human behavior and how people are so different in various settings. I had to pick up three passengers from the Maha Raja restaurant, an Indian restaurant. It is in Benfleet.

So, I reached the pickup point, and when they got inside the car, I got to know that they were doctors.

At that moment, I was like, "Wow, everyone's got a life at the end of the day."

Well, shaking the thought off, I focused on my job at hand. I had to take them to Benfleet, which was probably about a 20-minute drive.

They were a little drunk, talking loudly, shouting, putting music on the radio, and screaming. It was actually good to see them enjoying the night, carefree from the burdens of their day jobs. It was kind of an adventurous experience. I was a bit surprised to see them like that. You don't usually see doctors in such a state. When you think of them, you imagine them as tired, serious, and too focused on their job. And they are, but there is another side to their personality too, which I got to witness that day as they lived their nightlife. It made me laugh.

I was shocked when they told me they were doctors. I couldn't have guessed if they hadn't told me themselves. Then they started talking about their life, and that's when I realized that the life of people from other areas of work was different from becoming a doctor. And it took doctors a lot to become an ordinary person, much more than it takes for them to become doctors, it seemed. At that moment, they were just different people. They did not look like doctors at all. They were totally different.

I was happy to see that doctors do have a life at the end of the day, living beyond their professional roles. They might advise their patients against drinking during their work hours, but at night, when they're just normal human beings, they would drink to their heart's content.

This was evident when I picked up these three. Doctors on the loose, indeed!

CHAPTER 07

I hope you're enjoying these candid stories and finding it refreshing to be in the driver's seat for a change.

Here's another story I'd like to share with you. I once had a customer who booked a ride to a friend's wedding venue but surprisingly didn't book a return ride with me, which I had expected given the journey's length. The ride was long, so it was unusual for them not to book their return with the same company.

I started the ride and delivered them to the wedding venue around six o'clock. The event wrapped up between 10 and 11 o'clock, if I recall correctly. It was early December, so you can imagine how bitterly cold the nights were. As it turned out, they couldn't find any cabs nearby when the event ended. They likely assumed finding a cab in Chelmsford at that hour would be easy, but I knew better — at that time of night and in such cold, it was nearly impossible. It seemed they were unaware that they could book a return ride with the same company and driver when booking their pickup ride. So, they ended up stuck in Chelmsford.

They waited around an hour and a half, and to make matters worse, the venue closed, leaving them no option but to wait outside in the cold weather. Fortunately, they remembered they had the ABC company ride booking application and contacted them. They explained the whole situation to the company. Since they had reached out through the company, our customer representative was the first to respond, explaining how the booking system worked and that they could have easily booked a return ride to avoid any hassle.

When they asked ABC if they could book a return ride then, the representative assured them, saying, "We'll come and collect you." They were assured that ABC always prioritized its customers with pride and would come to pick them up even if they were stuck in Norwich, which is quite a long journey from Benfleet.

Upon inquiry, it turned out those people didn't know how the booking process worked, and being too drunk didn't help their situation. Anyway, the company contacted me as the nearest available driver in the area and instructed me to pick up the couple from the venue.

When I arrived there, I saw them standing in the cold, wearing clothes that barely offered any warmth. It was hard to believe they had been out there for over half an hour in minus 2-degree weather. I couldn't help but think about what might have happened if they hadn't thought to contact ABC company.

I immediately opened the door and urged them to get inside. They were shivering intensely. After they settled down a bit and their shivering eased, resembling less of a wet kitten, I asked them why they hadn't booked a return ride. They explained that they didn't know about this option and shared the rest of their story.

"I didn't think the company would actually send someone to pick us up at this hour," the guy said. I could tell that he was grateful.

I smiled and reassured them, "Don't worry. We'll always be there when you need us."

"Yes, I believe it now," the guy responded. "They had closed the venue and didn't even let us wait inside. It was so cold I couldn't think straight," he explained. I didn't know their names since the ride had been booked anonymously.

Finally, after hours of silent travel, we reached their destination. The couple's gratitude was overwhelming; they hugged me and even kissed me on the cheek, continuously thanking me and calling me a lifesaver. The moment was quite emotional. Although I'm not typically one for hugs, I didn't mind it this time. I was just happy to have been able to help. It was a fulfilling feeling.

That experience reinforced my faith in the good in the world and the appreciation people show when you go out of your way to help them in a difficult situation.

CHAPTER 08

This one is a scary one; at least, it was for me. If I say honestly, it is one of the worst experiences I have had as a cab driver. As usual, I was waiting for a ride, and I soon received one. The passengers were four boys, teenagers, as I remember, around 15 to eighteen years old. I had to pick them up from Tarpots in Benfleet.

So, I went to pick them up, and they got into the car. Three of them sat in the backseat, and one in the front beside me. I found them a bit unsettling since they were all wearing hoodies, and their faces were half covered by their hoods, so I couldn't really see their faces properly. I had a bad feeling about them but couldn't really do much at that time, so I just went with the flow.

I started driving and asked them again where they wanted to go since they hadn't answered the first time. They told me to go to Canvey High Street from Benfleet. It was around a six-mile journey. I put my meter on and started driving.

The guys behind me kept talking to each other, with the one beside me occasionally taking part in their conversation and turning in his seat to look at the boys in the back. I had no idea what they were talking about as I could only make out bits and pieces of their conversation, having my full focus on the road.

All I could gather was that they seemed to be planning something; exactly what and why, I couldn't tell. So, continuing the drive, I entered the town center. It was a 30-mile-per-hour zone, and I was cruising at about 28 mph. I always stay below the speed limit, usually at 28 or 29 mph, and never exceeding that. Twenty-eight miles per hour is a decent pace, especially since the road ahead was clear, allowing me to maintain a good speed comfortably.

The next moment completely caught me off guard; it seemed the boys planned to run away, likely because they didn't have the money to pay the fare. As we neared the town center, the boy sitting next to me suddenly opened the door and jumped out of the car. I hadn't engaged the child lock, thinking these teenagers were mature enough not to pull such a stunt.

I did have suspicions that they would try to run after we reached the destination since they looked dodgy and didn't seem to be old enough to have the kind of money to afford a cab ride. But never would I have thought of the possibility of them jumping out of a running car in the middle of the road.

When the first boy leaped from the front seat, I slowed the car in a panic, hoping he wouldn't be injured. This, however, provided an opportunity for the rest in the backseat. They seized the moment to make their escape, all except for one.

I got scared and didn't know what to do. I shouted and told them not to jump and that they would hurt themselves, but they didn't listen. I hadn't expected that they would all follow the first guy and could only see them in the rearview mirror.

There was one boy who didn't jump out and was stuck with me. I just said in shock, "Your friend just jumped out of a running vehicle! That's so irresponsible and dangerous. What were you guys thinking? You could have gotten killed or hurt pretty bad!"

"Look, I don't have money. The guys who have escaped have," the kid said.

"You guys need to pay, but that's not the concern right now," I said, exasperated. I didn't know if those guys were hurt or not. I knew I wasn't responsible for it if they were hurt because I was driving and didn't know they would do something like that.

Anyway, we reached the drop-off point, and I told the kid that he needed to pay. The meter showed 28 quids.

"No, no, I am not gonna pay!" the boy kept insisting.

"Well, then I have no other choice but to drop you back where I picked you from," I shrugged, turning the car around to head back to Benfleet to drop him off at the original pickup spot.

I wasn't upset; just worried about the three who had jumped out and hoped they were okay. I reported the incident to my company. They inquired if the boys were alright and whether I had called an ambulance. I explained that I couldn't see them from the car, so it seemed they likely escaped without injury. They appeared to be pros at this, having possibly done it several times before. Nonetheless, it didn't make their actions any less dangerous.

This experience was a real eye-opener for me regarding dealing with teenagers. It taught me that they can be quite troublesome if you're not constantly alert around them. Of course, the last kid, whom I dropped back, was very angry, but there wasn't much I could do about it. In a way, he was just facing the consequences of the stunt he and his friends tried to pull off. He was unfortunate to be the only one who got stuck with me, but perhaps he was lucky, too, considering he didn't jump and risk hurting himself in the process.

CHAPTER 09

Although I have good experiences with my customers most of the time, some memories bring me to tears even when I think about them. This is one such experience I had with a customer. I picked up a customer from the Elms Pub to take them to Benfleet and the Thundersley area, where I presumed their home was.

Knowing I was picking them up from a pub, I anticipated the passenger might be drunk. The passenger was a female, and although not too drunk, she was still quite tipsy. From the moment I picked her up, I sensed she was pretty sad, probably the reason she had been drinking at the pub alone, which isn't very common unless one is feeling down.

So, sensing she wasn't feeling okay, I asked her if she was okay. She was already talking to me, so I thought to ask her while mentioning that she seemed very upset. And as if my question had been the cue, whatever barrier was holding her tears back broke, and she started to cry.

I asked her again, which was met by laughter, which, of course, was anything but happy. This reaction made me realize she was deeply hurt and struggling to manage her emotions at the moment, appearing completely overwhelmed.

So when I reached the destination, I stopped the car and kept the lights and ignition on. I turned around to look at her and asked, "Hey, has anyone said something to you? Is there any way I can help you?"

I half expected an incoherent reply, but she actually opened up and told me her story. It revolved around her family and was related to COVID-19. She shared that she had a beautiful family: her mother, father, and one brother. They were a small family but happy. That was until Covid struck. Amidst the vaccination drive, they all got vaccinated, hoping it would shield them from the virus.

She had been reluctant about the vaccine, having researched and learned about it extensively. Despite her reservations and protests, her family went ahead with the vaccinations. Soon after, they began experiencing health issues. It started with her father, who had difficulty breathing and eventually passed away due to it. This was a shock to the family, and while they were grieving, they faced another trauma.

A few months after her father's death, her mother also started showing similar symptoms and soon passed away, followed by her brother, who also had health issues post-vaccination. She lost her entire family in a short span of time, all to a similar cause. I could only imagine the pain she was going through, losing her entire family. Her story made my heart ache, and despite my best efforts, I couldn't hold back my tears.

Being an emotional person, stories like these hit me hard. I didn't know what I could do or say to console her because her pain was unimaginable. Just thinking about going through something like that makes me cry. All I could do was listen to her, allowing her to let it all out and express her grief. I was glad she could share her story with me and hoped it helped ease her pain, even if just a little. Though there wasn't much I could do, I did my best to offer consolation.

Even though I knew it was hard for her to remain strong under such circumstances, I told her she was a strong woman and living with such a loss wasn't easy.

She nodded and took my hand, gently tapping on it as she said, "Please look after yourself. Don't have the COVID injection, please don't." Those words broke my heart. The medicine, intended to help people, had led her to believe it was the cause of her family's demise. I held a different opinion on the matter, but given the trauma she had experienced, I couldn't blame her for feeling that way. I simply nodded and helped her out of the car, walking her to her door. She hugged me before going inside.

On my walk back to the cab, I started crying. Her story had deeply affected me, making me very emotional. I was so heartbroken that I couldn't continue my night duty and went straight home.

CHAPTER 10

This experience was undeniably strange, mainly because it was so bizarre. It left me bewildered, questioning what exactly was happening. Honestly, I'm at a loss for words, but I'll continue sharing this story so you can make your own judgment.

I was near where ABC offices are based, headquartered in Benfleet. Right opposite our office is Zach Wilshere Pub. I had a job to pick some up from there and take them to a home in Benfleet. This was a very short journey, about five minutes long.

Upon arriving to pick up my passenger, I was met by an elderly woman who, although not too old, appeared to be around 55-56 years old. As she approached to enter the front seat, I noticed that she was drunk. While it's not unusual to come across drunk individuals, it's less common to see someone of her age in such a state, especially during the late hours. She was so drunk that she was having a hard time getting in the cab, so I helped her get inside.

Once I was settled in the driver's seat and had started the drive, keeping one hand on the gear stick and the other on the steering wheel of my manual car, I typically don't pay much attention to the passenger's actions since my focus is on the road. So, I was completely unprepared for what happened next.

Suddenly, the woman leaned forward and began to kiss and then lick my hand. I was momentarily paralyzed, shocked by the situation unfolding. Just so you know, I am around 29 years old, young, I suppose. So, it is natural for me to see people who are quite older than me with respect. Imagine my horror when I found that lady doing that while I was driving. It was crazy and embarrassing. Not to mention, I am a married man.

Nothing like that had ever happened to me, so I was kind of frozen for a few moments.

When it dawned on me what was happening, I turned to the lady and asked, "Excuse me, what are you doing?"

I asked politely, considering she was drunk and unaware of her actions. Her response was nothing more than an incoherent reply and a grunt. Thankfully, she leaned back into her seat, not attempting the action again.

We finally arrived at the destination and breathed a sigh of relief. But that was too soon for me to expect this was over, as the woman then invited me into her home. I was taken aback, and it was clear what she was trying to say and what her intentions were. I just told her that I was on duty and couldn't come with her. It was so strange to have an older woman hitting on you. She was at least 20-25 years my senior! So, all I could do was politely decline her advances and tell her the fare.

After paying, she didn't head to her house but approached the driver's side, opened the door, and, grabbing my arm, insisted, "Come with me now. Listen to me."

As if the situation wasn't bad already, she said, "I will pay you whatever you want."

I told her that she had already paid the fare and I didn't need any payment, hoping this would clarify that I was not interested in her proposition. However, she wouldn't take no for an answer and kept insisting I go with her.

I explained that I couldn't do that because I was married, hoping she would understand, but that didn't deter her. When all else failed, she began to touch the back of my neck and started kissing it. I moved her away and told her she needed to leave because I had work to do.

When she ignored my requests, I got out of the car, grabbed her arm, and walked her halfway to her door. It seemed she thought I had agreed to go with her, but as we neared her door, I left her and quickly returned to my car, drove off, and didn't look back.

Checking the rearview mirror, I saw she was watching my car but didn't follow, which was good since she was drunk, and I didn't want her to get hurt. After she was out of sight, I exhaled deeply, relieved that I had managed to escape the situation with my integrity intact.

CHAPTER 11

I know I've shared a few traumatic experiences in the previous chapters, but this one truly takes the cake. Even thinking about it as I write makes me shiver. I had to pick up a passenger from an island next to Benfleet, a place mentioned vaguely, without specifics on the exact location. I was supposed to follow directions from the passenger himself.

So, when I went to pick him up, he got into the car, and we began our journey. Something seemed very off about this guy. He was wearing a hoodie, his face concealed. Given it was dark, 2 in the morning, I couldn't really see his face, though I sensed he had covered it intentionally.

What made this passenger even more suspicious was that he sat right behind my seat, making it impossible for me to see what he was doing. Despite my suspicions, I maintained my composure and asked him where he wanted to go. I didn't talk much with this guy, as I usually would with my passengers, due to his unsettling aura.

He directed me to the drop-off location, and I continued driving. Shortly after, I felt him fiddling in his seat. Unable to see what he was doing since he was directly behind me, fear began to set in. His concealed face had already put me on edge. The only thing I could tell about him was that he was young, around 20-21 years old.

Despite my efforts to understand what was happening, I couldn't see anything. I didn't want to show that I was scared or suspicious, thinking it might provoke him. If he was really up to no good, alerting him would only worsen my situation.

I sat there, hoping the ride would end soon, but luck wasn't on my side. A few seconds later, the fiddling stopped, and the guy pulled something from his pocket. I feared it was a knife as I caught a glimpse of something glinting in the little light. The next second, he held it right next to my ear.

The chill of the object against my skin was enough to scare the life out of me. I immediately stopped the car near the garage of a BP petrol station, completely frozen in fear.

"Give me what you have got," the guy demanded.

Despite the panic setting in, I tried to remain calm, though I could hear my heart pounding violently. I only had 11 pounds in my pocket. Earlier that night, after earning more, I'd taken a brief trip home to drop off my earnings before taking another ride.

I handed him my bag and told him he could take whatever was inside. I told him that I had just started my shift and didn't have much on me.

For some reason, he seemed to think I was mocking him and became enraged. He pressed the object deeper into my skin, and that's when I realized it wasn't a knife. It didn't feel sharp against my skin, so I glanced in the mirror and saw that it was a gun.

The full understanding of the danger I was in hit me all at once, sending me into a panic. I started screaming, lost and desperate, pleading with him to take whatever he wanted and just leave me alone. I was mumbling incoherently, scared that he would kill me. I just wanted him to take anything that he wanted and leave me unharmed. Never in my life had I felt so scared. It was one of those moments when you feel, 'This is it. I'm going to die.'

I was scared that he would kill me because I didn't have much money. Then I thought about the Apple watch I was wearing and told him he could have it and 11 pounds in my bag. That was the most valuable asset I had at the moment to give him to save my life.

The guy kept insisting that I was lying and that I had more money hidden away. I assured him he could check my bag. Once he was convinced that I didn't have any more money, he demanded to know what the most expensive thing I had in the car was. I told him that it was the watch, but realizing it wasn't enough for him, I desperately offered my car, urging him to just take it and leave me be.

I attempted to appeal to his humanity, pleading, "Hey, look. I've got children, my friend. I'm here to make a living. I'm not here to die." Receiving no response, I continued, "I've got a family to provide for. If you kill me today, they won't have anyone to look after them." I was trying to convince him in any way possible, thinking about my family, my parents, and my children, fearing this might be the end.

I started thinking about my family and tried to convince him in so many different ways. "Please… you don't have to do this. This doesn't have to end this way. Please," I kept pleading. "I have got more money at home. I will give it to you. Just please don't kill me."

It seemed futile; the guy wasn't relenting. I had no other option but to resort to asking for help. I knew it was risky, but there was no other way. Aware of the risk, I discreetly pressed the emergency button on my phone, hoping it would connect me to the police. Fortunately, the brightness on my phone was set very low, so he couldn't see me using it.

I don't know what happened next. I was mumbling and kept trying to convince him not to kill me. I felt that he was about to pull the trigger and I was going to die. But he abruptly took the bag and whatever he could get his hands on and ran out of the car. I finally let out a sigh of relief and kept sitting in my car, thinking about what had just happened.

Soon after, the police arrived and questioned me about the incident. I recounted everything, and they began searching for the man. Unfortunately, they couldn't find him. It was quite late, so I decided to go home and leave the police to their work. However, the police never updated me on their search. It seemed they were unable to locate him.

This event shook me to the core, and I couldn't move past it for months. I don't know what made the guy reconsider his decision to shoot me. I was almost certain he was going to pull the trigger. Perhaps my mentions of my family and kids persuaded him? I'm not sure. I'm just grateful to be alive.

I stopped working altogether two or three months after this. The trauma was so intense that I decided to resign. My parents, terrified by the incident, wanted me to quit. When I went to the office to resign, my employers persuaded me to stay. They promised to conduct quick background checks on the passengers assigned to me to prevent such incidents in the future.

Even though I knew it wasn't entirely within their control, I chose to continue working. I became a bit more cautious around people and always remained vigilant for any suspicious behavior.

Better safe than sorry, I suppose. I didn't want to experience anything like that ever again.

CHAPTER 12

One time, I had to pick up a passenger who hadn't ordered the cab directly. It was from a BP petrol station, and they had requested a cab for a customer in Hadley. Upon arriving at the BP petrol station, I spotted a person standing outside. Assuming this was the customer I was to pick up, it didn't strike me as odd that the petrol pump staff might have ordered the ride on his behalf, so I didn't think why the individual hadn't booked the ride himself.

The man was imposing, likely around six and a half feet tall, with a robust build. He was carrying a lot of boards and a bag full of wine bottles. As he noticed the cab, he approached and took his seat in the front passenger seat. I greeted him and asked him how he was doing, to which he only grunted. The guy only grunted in response, making it clear that he wasn't interested in pleasantries. He seemed a bit tipsy, so that might be the reason he didn't want to talk.

Anyway, I asked him for his destination, and he directed me to South Benfleet, near Tar Pots. I understood his directions and started to drive. The journey was smooth until he began to tamper with items in the car. Initially, he fiddled with the door on his side before his curiosity led him to the holder next to my gear stick, which contained my personal belongings.

Although I found his behavior intrusive, I decided to remain silent and focus on driving. As we neared the halfway point of our journey, he seemed to grow more comfortable, continuously meddling with things in the car.

Despite my growing annoyance, I chose to keep my mouth shut. That was until he started to touch me. It wasn't anything inappropriate, but it definitely felt weird. I couldn't figure out what he was thinking. When he began touching my arm, that was enough for me. I asked him to stop, telling him he couldn't touch me like that. It was distracting, and while driving, it could be dangerous. Even if I wasn't driving, it still wouldn't be right.

I'm not sure if my reaction triggered something in him, but what he did next truly shocked me. He literally punched me in the face while I was driving. I was stunned! I stopped the car, held my hand to where he had hit me, and turned to look at him. What angered me more than the punch was that he wasn't even looking at me when I turned. He was clearly more drunk than I had initially thought.

I dialed the police as I got out of the car and walked to the passenger side.

I opened the door and told him, "Get out of my car. I'm not taking you."

The police were listening to everything over the call. I told the guy he had to pay me for the journey so far. I usually take payments through cards and keep a card reader in the car for that. Instead of listening to me, getting out of the car, and paying me, he picked up the card reader and threw it at me. Luckily, I ducked in time, and the reader hit the wall. It was badly smashed.

He then started to run around the car, taking his bottles of wine with him. I started to run after him, not knowing that the guy had more up his sleeves. He started to throw the wine bottles at me! Fortunately, I was away from the car; otherwise, he might have damaged it. The police were listening to everything through the call and dispatched officers to our location. I was still on the phone with them as I chased the guy. I had put the car hazard lights on so the police could spot us easily.

The police finally arrived and took charge. They put the guy down and took him. The following day, officers visited my home to inform me that the guy who attacked me was a senior police officer. I was shocked. How could a public service officer behave in such a manner? I didn't think being drunk was an excuse for such actions. Regardless of his intoxication, he should have behaved better.

The investigation into the officer began, and the police compensated me for the damaged card reader and the fare the man owed. I was disgusted by the senior officer's behavior who had attacked me. They are meant to protect us, yet here was one attacking a driver who was simply taking him home.

The incident just made me realize that you can't really tell much about a person by looking at them. It's troubling to think that someone capable of such violence could be part of the police force.

How could the government hire someone like that? I could have never known that he was a public police officer by his behavior. His actions were in direct contrast to what one would expect from a public officer, making me wonder just how unpredictable human behavior can be.

CHAPTER 13

This was a very strange experience that almost sent me into a panic. I had to pick up a passenger for a very short ride, which would have lasted only about 8-9 minutes. You might be wondering what could have possibly happened in such a brief span to make it worth sharing. Well, even though it was a really short ride, it turned out to be quite a hassle.

Here's what happened: I received a request to pick someone up from the woodlands near Elms Pub and take them to 44 Benfleet Park Road. Upon arrival, the scene was a bit chaotic, with many people around, making it difficult to identify my passenger.

However, I soon noticed a man approaching my car. He introduced himself as the one who had booked the cab, and I let him in, thinking we were ready to go. But then, he mentioned that more people were joining us. Looking outside, I was taken aback by the noisy crowd, among which was a couple arguing loudly, making their way to my car along with the guy's wife, who was sitting with me.

The man took his place in the front seat, with his wife directly behind me. The arguing couple approached; the man got in first, then forcefully pulled the woman into the car, seating her next to him. When the couple came, the guy got inside first and then pulled the girl forcefully inside and made her sit beside him. That's when I felt that something was wrong. The way the couple was screaming all the way to the cab and the way the guy pulled her was alarming.

I turned around to ask what was going on because the way they were treating the girl was a major red flag. The guy, her boyfriend, was screaming at her, saying, 'Get the fuck inside the car!' I tried again and asked the girl if everything was okay, but with the rest of them intervening, she couldn't say much and only kept resisting her boyfriend's hold.

The whole time, the guy sitting beside me, who I assumed was the father of the guy sitting in the back seat, stayed silent. I was shocked at how he could remain so calm, given the circumstances. "Calm down. Why are you screaming? Is everything okay?" I asked them in a firm tone, demanding an answer.

The father finally spoke up, saying, "Don't worry. Everything is okay. Just a little argument between the two." He tried to convince me, but I wasn't completely assured, though I couldn't say much more. Then, he indicated that I could start the ride. I let out a sigh of relief, hoping that the screaming would stop, and it did. But the way it happened was weird because one minute, the couple was screaming, and the next, they went dead silent.

Worried, I glanced in the rearview mirror and saw that the girl was crying, actually sobbing. Shaking my head, I started to drive, relieved that the journey was short and I wouldn't have to deal with this drama for long. However, that relief was short-lived. The couple began to argue again, this time even more intensely.

The guy's mother also started to scream at the girl. Since I was driving, I couldn't do much to intervene or fully understand what was happening behind me. At first, I didn't realize they had started to physically fight. My focus was on the road, and I thought that they were just arguing and screaming. But I was wrong.

The situation escalated quickly; the guy and his girlfriend had gone mad, hitting each other pretty badly. They were slapping, punching, and pushing each other, completely disregarding the fact that they were in a cab.

That's when I'd had enough and started to yell at them, "What are you guys doing?" Concerned for the girl, I directly addressed her, "Are you okay? What's the matter? Why are you guys fighting? What happened?" It was then the girl told me, "No. Nothing is okay. They are harassing me, and they have been beating me." After saying that, she began to cry, which only added to my concern for her.

Turning to her boyfriend, I demanded, "Is she telling the truth? That's not right. That's unacceptable!" I continued to lecture the guy, making it clear that their behavior, beating and mistreating the girl, was wrong. My attention was split between what was going on in the car and the road, so I was taken by surprise by what happened next.

The girl suddenly unlocked the door, seemingly intending to jump out while the car was moving at 30 miles per hour. My car alerted me with a beep when the door was unlocked, which tipped me off to her foolish and desperate plan. She was seated diagonally behind me, so I was able to reach her. My instincts kicked in, and I reacted fast, grabbing her arm just as she opened the door and pressing the brake to slow the car down.

From that point on, it all got crazier. Despite her emotional state and attempts to resist, I was adamant about stopping her from jumping out of the moving car. She was emotional, I knew, and was going to get herself hurt pretty bad if I hadn't stopped her. Surprisingly, the mother and her son seemed indifferent to her attempts. The mother even began to hit the girl with any object she could get her hands on, with her son joining in on the abuse.

We had almost reached the destination, only a right turn away from the drop-off point. The chaos continued, and by that point, the guy's parents became even more apparent—they seemed to be on his side, encouraging rather than stopping him. I still didn't know what it was all about and just wanted to finish the ride.

The guy had locked the door back by the time we had reached the drop-off. When the car stopped, the girl didn't waste a second and got out of the car, screaming at the top of her lungs. This attracted the attention of bystanders, who gathered around to witness the commotion caused by the family. The father, seemingly unphased by the unfolding drama, handed me the fare. I checked it, but it was all sorts of change, so I couldn't exactly count the amount right away. I was too distracted by what was happening.

I was afraid that they might hurt the girl again, so I immediately called the police and told them about the incident. They assured me that they would handle the matter from there and that I didn't have to worry about it.

I was very disturbed by the whole episode. I really hoped that the police were able to figure out what was the matter and had helped the girl. She could have died had she jumped out of the car. Thankfully, I acted in time and was able to stop her.

This was one of the most memorable rides I had ever taken, and not in a good way. It was scary even though the journey was supposed to be only 8 minutes long, but the chaos caused by the guy and his parents made it one of the most distressing short trips I had taken.

CHAPTER 14

There is another story I would like to share with you. This one is particularly interesting because of an incident that got published in an article where I was named an ABC hero. When they posted that article, I created an account on TikTok and uploaded it there as well. I go by the name Mo on TikTok, just in case you want to check it out.

When this particular incident happened, I knew it was something you don't experience every day. However, I never imagined that I would be approached for an interview about the whole ordeal and be honored with the title of an "ABC hero." The publication of that article inspired me to think about writing a book based on my experiences as a taxi driver, intending to include this story. It's not that I believe I should brag about my story being published, but I thought that people could learn a lot from my experience, just as I did.

So, what happened was I had a ride to pick up someone from South Benfleet and take them to Canvey Island. It was a short journey, probably about five miles. When I picked up these customers, they were just so happy to meet me. They loved the way I approached them and how I spoke to them. I always appreciate when people recognize politeness and generosity, so it was a good feeling. The passengers were two boys and two girls, and I had picked them up around 11 o'clock.

It was Saturday night, a very busy and important day, considering there was a lot of work, with people finally getting time to go out and enjoy their weekend. It's one of those days when drivers usually don't want to get stuck with anything that would delay their work and affect their income. They aim to make as much money as possible on these nights and usually won't stop for anything. I, on the other hand, don't think the same way. Although extra money is always a good thing, I would gladly sacrifice it if it meant stopping when I sensed something wrong happening or someone in need of help. I would stop and pause to find out what was happening and, if necessary, seek out the police.

So, the young people I picked up were very nice, making for a pleasant ride. I was driving at my usual pace when, all of a sudden, a Ford vehicle abruptly pulled out onto the road, driving rashly. Fortunately, my car was behind it, so we avoided any damage. Initially, I couldn't see the driver clearly as they were driving quite recklessly, even on the wrong side of the road. This wasn't a rare sight on Saturday nights, with many rash drivers around, often drunk and careless about safety. But this instance was very alarming.

As if the reckless driving wasn't frightening enough, I noticed two girls walking towards the car, or rather, the car driving towards them. At first, it seemed the driver was trying to impress them with his 'skills,' which I found utterly foolish. However, it soon became clear that he wasn't trying to show off; he was simply drunk and out of control.

I had a flashlight in my car, so I quickly grabbed it and started flashing it towards him, hoping he would notice and stop. The passengers in my car joined in, trying to warn the girls to move out of the way and urging the driver to stop. But the driver, clearly very drunk, ignored our attempts to get his attention. I doubted he could even hear us, given his state.

Fortunately, our flashing lights and shouts caught the girls' attention, and they jumped out of the way just in time, narrowly avoiding a disastrous collision. The driver seemed oblivious to the near-miss and continued driving like a maniac. Knowing he was a danger to others, I decided to follow his car with my passengers still onboard.

Holding my flashlight and shouting as loudly as I could, I continued my attempts to stop him. Driving fast yet carefully, since I was behind him, I remained aware of the safety of my passengers despite the urgency. Although it was still risky, I knew that it had to be done, or else he would have killed someone. It was 11 PM, and the roadsides were likely crowded with people near pubs and clubs.

Eventually, when I managed to get close enough, I sounded a loud horn and stopped my car diagonally next to his. The combination of flashing lights and screaming seemed to shake him out of his drunken haze, and he slowed down, giving me a chance to intercept him. After turning off my car, I approached his vehicle. He didn't resist when I asked him to get out, but upon doing so, he collapsed to the ground, unable to stand. I couldn't help but shake my head at his recklessness. It was evident he had no idea of his actions or the danger he posed, and had I not stopped him, he could have caused a tragedy in the crowded area not far ahead.

While I was dealing with the drunk driver, my customers called the police. The police arrived at the scene after I had left and, after some investigation, approximated that he would have probably killed around 20 people had he not been stopped. I was appalled when I got to know about this and thanked God that I was able to stop him in time.

So, after the police had been called, I told my customers that it was better to get this drunk guy dropped at home because he clearly couldn't drive in that state. I didn't want to risk the possibility of him getting behind the wheel again. So, I took the guy in my cab and asked him where he lived. He managed to tell me, as best as he could, in his slurred, drunk tone. However, a bit later, I realized that I was making a mistake by taking him with me. The police should have taken care of him for rash driving and putting people's lives at risk. So, I decided to go against my initial plan and waited for the police to arrive instead.

My customers were still with me in the car as I drove the drunk guy with us. I felt bad for putting them through this ordeal, but they said that it was okay. They appreciated my efforts to prevent a potentially horrible accident and decided to stay with me.

The police arrived after some time and took the guy with them. I continued with my work for the rest of the evening after dropping those customers at their destination. They offered money to pay the fare, but I felt it wouldn't be fair to them after all the commotion caused by the drunk driver.

Moreover, it was bitterly cold outside, yet they stayed with me the entire time until the driver was taken away by the police. I told them that I wouldn't be charging them for the ride, but they insisted on paying. They didn't just cover the fare; they also gave me an extra 20 pounds as a token of appreciation for my bravery. I expressed my gratitude for their understanding and support throughout the entire ordeal. They simply smiled at me and dismissed their actions as nothing, asserting that I was the real hero. I thanked them once more for their kindness before driving away.

The following day, I received a phone call from the ABC office asking me to come to the office immediately. When I reached there, I was told that some publishers wanted to talk to me about last night's incident. While it was indeed a proud moment for me to be recognized for my efforts, my greater pride was having been able to save lives. Even if my story had not been featured in that article, I would still hold pride in having played my part as a responsible citizen and a decent human being.

CHAPTER 15

Okay, so this is a crazy story, but one that I'm very proud of. It was a chaotic ride, to be honest, but afterward, I felt so happy to have been able to help someone. Looking back on this incident, I believe that if any other driver had been in my place that day with that passenger, they might have handled it differently. They probably wouldn't have known what to do. Let me share with you what exactly happened.

As usual, I had a job to pick someone up from Thundersley Park Road and take them to Southern Hospital. The passenger's name was Syrah, and I needed to drop her off at Southend Hospital. Judging by the location, I suspected it might be some sort of emergency, so I hurried to the pickup spot. When I saw the passenger approaching the car, I noticed she was heavily pregnant, probably due in a few days.

However, my assumptions were quickly proven wrong when I saw her in pain, tears rolling down her face. It was clear she was already in labor and could give birth at any minute.

I was initially panicked and worried upon seeing her condition, but I knew I had a job to do—a very important one at that. So I composed myself as she got into the back of my vehicle. Through her pained voice, she told me she urgently needed to get to the emergency department at Southend Hospital.

"Please, can you hurry?" she requested.

Of course, sensing the urgency, I knew I had to drive fast while ensuring her safety throughout the journey. When I activated the navigation app, it showed that the hospital wasn't too far away, but the traffic looked bad. It was estimated that we would reach the hospital in 38 minutes due to the traffic conditions. It was school time, typically a rush hour, which explained the congestion.

Despite having no experience with childbirth, I could tell by her pain that she was very close to giving birth. I knew we couldn't wait 38 minutes; the baby wouldn't wait. I was initially unsure what to do, but after a few calming breaths and some quick thinking, I decided to take alternative routes through inner roads that were usually clear during these hours. It was the only option that came to mind at the moment. I realized that if I didn't hurry, both her baby's life and her own could be in danger. I didn't want to take that risk.

So, I veered off the suggested route in the app and took the inner roads, hoping they would offer a shortcut. I was driving as quickly as I could while still trying to keep my passenger safe, but then nature threw us another curveball. Five minutes into the drive, the woman told me her water had broken. Although I didn't fully understand what that meant, her screams and panting made it clear that we were running out of time and the baby was coming soon. I was panicking a bit myself but kept driving.

Normally, I would never speed, but I knew this was a matter of life and death, so I pressed the pedal harder and sped up to 35 miles per hour. The frontage roads are usually empty but full of bumps, so I had to slow down several times to navigate them carefully. I had my hazard lights on so other drivers would know I was speeding because of an emergency.

Finally, I managed to get her to the hospital without getting stuck in traffic. Upon arrival, the first thing I did was call for an attendant to bring Syrah a wheelchair. The nurses assisted me as I informed them that her water had broken. The staff was very cooperative, and she was quickly inside the hospital, hopefully receiving the care she needed. I was so worried about her that I forgot to end my ride in the app or even take the keys out of the ignition. At that moment, the fare was the last thing on my mind.

After ensuring she was taken care of, I returned to my car to check the backseat, which obviously needed some deep cleaning. I ended up spending 70 pounds on getting the seats and floor cleaned. Even though that ride cost me 70 pounds and made me no money, I felt relieved and satisfied knowing I had helped someone and possibly saved a life. So, I left my car to be cleaned and went back home that day after informing my company.

The next day, I received a call from the office telling me that I needed to come in as soon as possible. When I arrived, I was surprised with a flower bouquet, a box of chocolates, and an envelope. Megan, one of the employees, informed me that they were sent for me. "Oh, this is interesting," I thought.

I asked her who sent them, but she didn't know. She only mentioned that a man had dropped them off. After asking around the office, I found out it was Syrah's husband. I opened the envelope that came with the gifts and found a note along with 100 pounds. Although this didn't cover the money I lost from not taking more rides, it did cover the cleaning expense and the fare for that particular ride, with 10 pounds to spare. Although I was okay with not being paid, given the circumstances, I was touched by their thoughtfulness in making sure to compensate me.

I read the note that was in the envelope, and it said: "Can you please call us when you receive this?" It also had a number written on it.

After reading the note, I went back to my vehicle and decided to make the call. The husband answered, greeting me warmly and expressing his gratitude for my service. He told me, "You saved my wife and our child. You saved our child." I was a bit shocked. I knew that rushing her to the hospital was the right thing to do, but saving the child? That was more than I had realized. He explained that the doctors had said if she had been even a few minutes later, they might have lost the baby. The umbilical cord had been wrapped around the baby's neck, and any further delay could have led to suffocation.

The conversation was lengthy, filled with his thanks. I was glad to have helped the couple and played a part in their joy. When I returned to the office, it turned out they had already been informed about the situation. As I walked in, they praised me and gave me pats on the shoulder, telling me that customers always had good things to say about me and that I was very dedicated to my job.

It was a unique feeling. I had never witnessed or experienced such a situation and had no clue what to do initially. I just followed my instincts and got my passenger to her destination in time. The journey, supposed to take 38 minutes, I managed to cover in only 14 minutes—a new record for me, spurred by the urgency of the situation and a rush of adrenaline. Yet, I made sure to ensure the safety of both the mother and her baby by carefully avoiding bumps and obstacles along the way. It was indeed an accomplishment.

Feeling immensely happy, I shared the story with my family, who were incredibly proud of me. This experience is one of those that reminds me why this job is so important. It might not seem like much to some, but it can indeed help save lives when needed.

CHAPTER 16

This one was a funny experience and a bit emotional as well. I live in England, so football matches are a big deal here. This incident occurred during the 2022 World Cup—imagine the hype. It was the semifinal between England and France, with the winner qualifying for the final match. For us cab drivers, it was the busiest day of the year as everyone was rushing to pubs, clubs, and houses to watch the game. Despite the chaos, I loved the vibe. Everyone was happy and excited about the match, though it turned stressful during the final hours when the outcome was about to be determined.

I was working that night and had an app open on my car screen that updated the scores every now and then. So, even though I couldn't watch the entire match, I followed the scores to stay informed. I could only follow scores since there were so many customers to pick up from various locations. If you watched that match, you'd remember the outcome. If not, England lost that night. Everyone had hoped England would reach the final, but France beat it to it. It was a sad night for all. You could see the disappointment on people's faces.

As for me, it was a crazy night in terms of the types of customers I had during pickups, but overall, I had a good time. Until the match was over, everything ran smoothly, and the night felt like a festival, with people drinking, laughing, and enjoying themselves. But as the match neared its end, it was time for us to pick up customers and take them home, and everyone was emotional. Not a single customer seemed anything but upset when I picked them up, and some were absolutely furious about losing the match.

Let me share an incident with you about one such customer. He was the third customer I picked up, and he sat in the front with me. As I drove him home, he was so angry about the loss that he started punching my dashboard, slamming the gear stick, and shouting, "Why did Kane miss that penalty?" He even started swearing at Kane, completely losing it. I tried to calm him down, saying, "My friend, it's okay. Next time, we'll win. There's no need to punch my dashboard; you're damaging my vehicle. You need to calm down." But he just kept shouting all the way to his house. It was madness, but also hilarious. He stormed into his house, still very angry and upset.

Then, I picked up my next customer right after dropping off the previous one. He got in with his girlfriend and sat right behind me. To my surprise, the man was crying. Why? Because England had lost the match! It was quite a sight; I understand being upset, but crying? That seemed to take it to another level. He was a grown, mature man, and yet there he was, in tears. That day, I truly realized just how deeply English people feel about football. Trying to console him, I said, "Hey, don't worry. We'll win next time." But this only made things worse, and he burst into louder tears. I offered him some tissues, unsure of what else I could say to calm him down. He was crying really bad and had a runny nose. I am not exaggerating.

His girlfriend appeared a bit lost herself, seeing her boyfriend so distraught over a game. She kept reassuring him, "Don't worry, we will win next time," but nothing seemed to console him. Despite feeling sorry for him, I couldn't help but find the situation somewhat amusing. It was getting hard to keep a straight face.

My next passengers were two best friends, one supporting France and the other England. You can imagine the tension: two best friends rooting for opposing teams? Disaster! Believe it or not, by the time the match was over, they were swearing at each other. One was over the moon with France's win, the other devastated by England's loss. It was just a match; there was no need to fight over it! They continued bickering about the game, throwing insults back and forth until they finally went silent, but it was clear that they were mad at each other. I dropped them off and could only shake my head at the madness I'd witnessed that night.

Next, I picked up a married couple, one supporting England and the other France. Fortunately, they were not arguing but instead laughing and teasing each other playfully. The husband kept taunting his wife, "You lost," while she playfully rolled her eyes, brushing it off. "The French did it. France did it. We're going to get the cup now, yeah!" he boasted. "Yeah, it was your lucky day," she retorted. Their interaction was a refreshing change from the intense emotions I had seen earlier that night.

You won't believe what one of my customers showed me that night. After expressing how upset he was over the match, he asked me, "Can I show you something?" Curious, I agreed and followed him to the back of his house, which led to a garden. There, he showed me a pile of TVs he had smashed.

"That's how upset I get when we lose," he explained. It seemed to me that he was more invested in league teams rather than just England, and some TVs were broken during other matches. But clearly, he was also upset over that night's game, which he had watched at the pub where I picked him up. Obviously, he couldn't smash a TV there.

It was an unforgettable night, filled with customers each handling their disappointment over the match in their own unique ways. For me, the experience was both crazy and amusing. One thing became clear: deep down, when it came to their country, they were all the same—emotional, sensitive, and fiercely patriotic!

CHAPTER 17

This incident is one of the most recent. I had a job to pick someone up from the Bread and Cheese Pub in Benfleet, a well-known place. The job was a 'direct' one, meaning I wasn't given specific details about the customer. When I arrived, I found around 15 or 16 people surrounding one woman. I didn't know who my customer was because the job didn't mention her name.

The scene was quite chaotic. This woman, who was extremely drunk, was at the center of attention. These people were trying to ensure she got home safely, which is why they had called a cab. She seemed to think she was being harassed because of how they were crowding around her and attempting to help her into my car. It felt unbelievable, almost ridiculous, the way they were handling her. I was worried and thought, 'Oh, my goodness, this is unbelievable.'

Then, I opened my window and said, 'Guys, chill out. It's okay. This is part of my daily routine. She's my customer, and I'll take her home safely. You don't need to traumatize her or me. Just be gentle with her and leave it to me. I'll handle this, okay?'

Next thing I knew, some random guy from the crowd got into my car and sat next to the woman, insisting he would accompany her to ensure she got home safely. It was pretty clear that this guy didn't even know the woman. I'm not sure if he realized it, but he was a complete stranger to her, yet he claimed he could ensure her safety better than me—a licensed cab driver. I couldn't understand why he thought he was a more reliable option when he said, 'I will go with her. She is not safe with a cab driver."

I was appalled by his audacity when he said that. I asked him, "Do you even know her name?" He said no, which I already suspected. I told him, "That's it. You have no right to be here or to take her home, so get out of my car." However, he was adamant about accompanying her all the way to her home to ensure she arrived "safely." I wasn't willing to take the risk of having him in the car as they were in the backseat, and I couldn't intervene while driving if something happened during the journey. I made it clear that I couldn't allow him to come along because it was too easy for a stranger to take advantage of a drunk woman.

The woman, though drunk, confirmed to me that she didn't know the man when I asked her. I needed her confirmation to be sure that I was doing the right thing by wanting to kick the man out. When he wouldn't listen, I stepped out of the car, explained the situation to some people from the crowd, and asked for their assistance in removing him. Fortunately, they helped me, and they literally pulled the man out of the car as he resisted.

I asked one of those people to give me their phone number so I could inform them when I had safely dropped the woman off at her home. Then, I got back into the car and started the ride. It wasn't meant to be a long ride, but as I was unfamiliar with the destination and mostly relied on the directions the woman provided, it took us 40 minutes to reach her place. She was extremely drunk, which made it difficult for her to remember the route and direct me. Once we arrived, she staggered out of the car. I got out and helped her into her house. After ensuring she was safe, I left.

The entire situation was quite overwhelming for me, especially dealing with the stranger who kept insisting on accompanying the woman. I was also a bit offended. How could he question my integrity as a driver? In our profession, companies don't grant us a license until we've proven our honesty. We undergo numerous courses and tests, and only then are we deemed fit to transport customers and trusted with their safety. Taking drunk people home safely is routine for us; we do it every day.

The point I'm making is that it's generally safer to trust a cab driver than a complete stranger who insists on taking you home under the guise of "safety." You never know what could happen. Cab service companies conduct thorough background checks on their drivers and monitor their whereabouts while on the job. It's much easier to track a cab driver than a complete stranger if something goes wrong.

Honestly, I find local cab services to be more reliable than Uber. Uber doesn't conduct as rigorous background checks on their drivers. I'm not saying it's a bad service or that I'm against it—after all, I use these services, too. However, from my experience, local cabs seem more reliable. Once, I booked an Uber for a friend, but it wasn't a good experience. The driver fell asleep while driving on the motorway, which was incredibly dangerous for both the driver and the passengers. My friend had to throw water on his face to keep him awake.

This story is just a reminder of how seriously we take our responsibilities. I've never left a customer stranded, regardless of the situation. Even after reaching their destination, I make sure they are inside their home before I leave. I know I don't have to do these little things, but they make a significant difference in the quality of service we provide. More importantly, I believe it's my duty as a human being to ensure that my customers get home safe and sound.

CHAPTER 18

Sometimes, in the journey of life, you meet people from whom you learn, and at times, you teach them. My job allows me to meet people from all walks of life, and I always learn a thing or two from each encounter. With every ride, I am exposed to something new, no matter how small or trivial it might seem. This is one such incident where I learned a valuable lesson from a customer.

I had to pick someone up from High Road in Benfleet and drop them off in Eastwood. The customer ID showed his name, Joe. When I arrived, he sat in the backseat. I greeted him, and we started the ride. During the journey, he talked to me, and he seemed like a good guy—very smart, honestly. I could tell he was brought up well by the way he spoke.

I love it when my customers match my energy as I ask questions and try to ensure everyone has a good time during the journey. Joe was one such customer. He responded sensibly as I asked him about his day.

As the conversation continued, he began to share his life story. He told me he was a homeless man who had spent quite some time living on the streets. I was baffled because he was far from what I would picture a homeless person to be. I understand that some homeless people do manage to improve their life situations, but this man seemed extraordinary. I couldn't imagine he had once been homeless as he appeared very well-educated and sensible.

Don't get me wrong: I am not saying that homeless people aren't intelligent or sensible, but not many are able to transform their lives so remarkably. As he shared his past, he mentioned that he had never talked about it with anyone else, and I was the first person he felt he could open up to. He felt at ease with me, and knowing that made me incredibly happy. I don't know if you can understand my feelings, but there's something profoundly rewarding about being able to offer an ear and let someone speak their heart out.

He then told me about a friend of his from that time named Luke, who used to sleep beside him on the streets. What he shared next was heartbreaking. One night, while they were sleeping near a pub, a drunk man approached them. They were in their sleeping bags, the ones that you have to zip up to seal in warmth, making it hard to escape quickly. In his drunken stupor, the man set Luke's sleeping bag on fire. By the time they realized what was happening, it was too late. The fire spread rapidly, and Luke died on the spot.

Though the man who set the fire was arrested and sentenced to life in prison, Joe had lost his best friend. I felt so deeply saddened by his story that I found myself at a loss for words. Joe then said, "I was lucky that day that my bag didn't catch fire. I could have died too, but I was lucky to survive."

Then, he continued to share his experiences as a homeless person, telling me how rough life had been for him back then. I asked how long he had been living on the streets, and I was shocked to learn that he had been homeless for eight years! I hadn't expected it to be that long, but knowing this only increased my respect for him.

I then asked how he managed to escape that situation. He told me that one Christmas, he was approached by a man who said they looked after homeless people in the area. It was like a community built for homeless individuals that offered them some money to help better their lives. This man gave him £5,000, some clothes, food, and a place to live.

That sounded like an absolute miracle to me, and I was very emotional hearing it. Although it was sad to learn about the tough life he had endured for eight years, losing his friend and surviving the bitter cold on the streets, I was glad that life had finally turned around for him. Life gave him a chance, and he seized it to make a change. And I could see that he had succeeded in doing so.

I was deeply inspired by his story, and it made me reflect on the blessings in my life. I've had my share of good and bad days, but hearing what he endured for so long made me think twice before complaining about anything. He taught me that no matter how difficult things become, there's always hope for a better tomorrow.

When we reached his destination, I refused to take the fare for the ride. I told him, "I'm not going to charge you. You're a very good person, and you've inspired me so much. This ride is on me."

I kept insisting, but he was adamant, saying, "You've earned it, so you should take it. I appreciate your offer, but I would feel better if you take the money."

I understood and respected his sentiments and accepted the money. Not only did he pay the fare, but he also gave an extra 3 pounds as a tip. I thanked him for the tip, but I was even more grateful for him sharing his story with me and imparting such a valuable lesson about life.

READERS, WE HAVE ARRIVED AT YOUR DESTINATION!

Being a driver might seem like an easy job, but it's not—and I only realized this after I started working as a cab driver. Whatever I experience on this journey always presents two perspectives: one from my customers and one from me. Either way, I find it to be an adventurous and fun experience for both of us; at least, I try to make it one for my customers. These experiences are happy, sad, terrifying, shocking, and simply amazing. I don't believe I would have ever encountered such a diverse range of experiences if I were only doing an office job. Though I love my office job as well, the freedom that comes with cab driving is unmatched. And as fun as it is, I must say again, it is not an easy job. As I mentioned, the customers, or passersby, may think it is easy, but that's their perspective. Mine, being on the road all night, reveals a whole new world out there.

I'm 29 years old, but I've learned so much from being a taxi driver that one might think I have lived 50 years already. Probably because I have met so many people from various ages and professions, learning different things from each of them. I don't believe many people get the chance to meet so many diverse individuals, talk to them, and learn a thing or two in a single day like I do. I think it is a privilege in its own right, so I do my job with pride.

This job has also transformed me as a person. I've become more patient, more considerate of others' feelings, and better at managing my time. I mean, I do my office job during the day and drive at night without wearing myself out. Yes, it's a bit tiring at times, but it's more rewarding. I've also become a better family member. I used to get annoyed easily, but having met so many people and learned their stories, I am more understanding of their feelings and situations. I no longer get frustrated so easily. I mean, I've met the nastiest and the nicest people as my customers and have had to regulate my emotions accordingly. I can't lash out at the difficult ones, no matter their behavior. As a driver, it's my duty to remain polite with them, no matter how challenging the situation becomes. This has made me think: if I can keep my emotions in check with them, I can certainly do the same with my family and friends.

In short, I get to experience the world from my small cab. I meet people from all walks of life—the poorest, the richest, the youngest, and the oldest. I've learned to handle all these interactions in the best way possible. I've come across traumatic scenes and witnessed moments of joy and entertainment. So, in my opinion, it's nothing short of a rollercoaster ride where you have to stay calm and not panic, no matter what situation you face along the way.

Taxi driving as a career is tough. You need to be very patient and kind and sometimes selfless, too. You can't just leave a passenger in the middle of a ride if you feel tired. Once you've committed, you have to ensure your customer safely reach their destination, and then you can sign off. That's the level of responsibility expected of you.

So, this is how I roll at night: behind the steering wheel, with a cup of cappuccino before I start my shift to stay alert all night. It's not easy sacrificing your sleep to earn a few extra bucks for your family, but at the end of the day, it's all worth it. However, if you're going to do this job, do it with integrity. You have to be very careful because you don't know these people, and you don't know what might happen during the journey. Your customer could be anyone, and you should expect the unexpected from them. But you must understand what is expected of you as a driver so that you can ensure the journey, even if it's just for a short while, ends safely and happily for both you and your customer.

I know some taxi drivers who are not very patient or calm. Fortunately, I am not one of them. So, if you happen to get me as your driver around Benfleet, you're in for a very lively conversation throughout the journey—that I can assure you of!

For now, our ride together comes to an end here. I hope you enjoyed reading about these experiences as much as I enjoyed sharing them with you. Until next time, take care and keep journeying through life's adventures!

ABOUT THE AUTHOR

Mohammad Ali Shah is a multifaceted individual balancing two professions: by day, he's an accountant, and by night, he's a cab driver. Beyond his professional roles, Mohammad is a devoted father to four children and a loving husband to his beautiful wife. Coming from a large family of nine siblings, Mohammad values the importance of community and giving back, evident through his family's annual charity events.

Born in Ishoj, Denmark, Mohammad has spent his entire life in England, near the picturesque Southend-on-Sea. Despite his academic background in Accounting & Finance, Mohammad never anticipated becoming an author. However, he has found his calling in writing, eager to share the diverse experiences and perspectives of life. Mohammad looks forward to releasing the second part of his book, where he delves deeper into the complexities of existence.